Ronit & Jamil

Ronit & Jamil

Pamela L. Laskin

KATHERINE TEGEN BOOKS
An Imprint of HarperCollinsPublishers

"No Place to Hide" from *Elemental Poems* by Tommy Olofsson. Copyright © 1995 by White Pine Press. Reprinted by permission of White Pine Press.
"The Music We Are" from *Rumi: The Book of Love: Poems of Ecstasy and Longing*, translated by Coleman Barks. Copyright © 2003 by Coleman Barks. Reprinted by permission of HarperOne.
"Lesson from the Kama Sutra," "Mural," "A Rhyme for the Odes," and "Who Am I Without Exile," from *Unfortunately, It Was Paradise: Selected Poems* by Mahmoud Darwish. Copyright © 2003, 2013 by The Regents of the University of California. Reprinted by permission of University of California Press.
"Your Village" from *Eyes, Stones* by Elana Bell. Reprinted by permission of LSU Press. Copyright © 2012 by Elana Bell.

Acknowledgment is made to the following publications in which these poems by the author appeared or will soon be appearing:

"What I Love." www.bestpoem.com/2014
"Imagine: The Pharmacist's Profession." *Talisman*. January 2015
"It's Complicated," "No More," "Through the Window," "Where I'm From," "You Just Don't Understand." *Sukoon*

Katherine Tegen Books is an imprint of HarperCollins Publishers.

Ronit & Jamil
 For information address HarperCollins Children's Books, a division of HarperCollins Publishers, 195 Broadway, New York, NY 10007.
www.epicreads.com

Library of Congress Control Number: 2016949687
ISBN 978-0-06-245854-4

Typography by Carla Weise
17 18 19 20 21 PC/LSCH 10 9 8 7 6 5 4 3 2 1
❖
First Edition

To Ira—my beginning, middle, and ending

To Ella—you have awakened a world of possibilities

INTRODUCTION

RONIT & JAMIL IS SET IN PRESENT-DAY ISRAEL, A REGION IN the Middle East facing many challenges and a conflict with roots dating back to the formation of the Jewish state. However, conflict has existed in this region for many generations. This book does not focus on the historical claims to this land, but rather how the formation of Israel in 1947 sparked a conflict that continues today.

The 1947 UN General Assembly partitioned Palestine into two states, one Jewish and one Arab. Despite this resolution, an uprising began almost immediately, which ultimately resulted in an armistice agreement and the formation of three separate entities:

Israel; Jordan, which occupied East Jerusalem; and the hill country of central Palestine (the West Bank). Some Arab Israelis fled at this time, though some remained in Israel, not always with the same rights as Israeli citizens. In 1967, war broke out in the area, and Israel acquired additional land in this region. The UN Security Council's solution to this acquisition did not satisfy the Palestinian Arabs, who felt they had a right to return to their homeland. Whose land is this? That is the central question.

There is no right or wrong here, but there are key issues that remain: mutual recognition; security; control of Jerusalem, where both sides have historic claims; Israeli settlements; Palestinian right of return. There continues to be violence here, where—in truth—some people would love to see a resolution in which the two sides, Palestine and Israel, can coexist.

This book is about young people and their commitment to transcend the endless conflicts that continue to plague this area.

READER'S NOTE

THERE ARE SEVERAL REFERENCES TO A "FENCE" THROUGHOUT the book. This is actually a separation barrier—being built by Israel—that runs near the "Green Line" between Israel and the West Bank. The premise behind it is that it would prevent terrorists from entering Israel proper; however, there is much controversy surrounding this structure.

Let's be the same wound
if we must bleed.
Let's fight side by side,
even if the enemy
is ourselves: I am yours,
you are mine.
—*Tommy Olofsson*

Ronit

I go with him to work, my Abba
it's summer
heat
a leech
an ulcer.

Papa has pills, elixirs
to heal the sick, the wounded,

first stop
Mohammed in East Jerusalem.
"Damn good doctor," he tells me.

"Oh, he has a son.
Don't look at him."

Jamil

I go with him to work
my Abi,
sizzling summer heat
clings to my back.

He waits for Chaim, the pharmacist,
to give him medicines—
magic
to heal the sick, the wounded.

"A decent man," Abi says.
"Oh, he has a daughter.
Don't look at her."

ACT I

Naming Things

To Work

I am my father's son
though I am a girl,
but as firstborn
of three,
he gives me power like an amulet
cherishes my voice
like it's the Bible,
asks my opinion
like it's a prize,
but he still doesn't want to hear
that I don't want to go to the army.
He takes me to his work
so I can see the way things are.

To Work

You are the sun of my heart
for you I burn
Abi chants
like a prayer
all the while questioning
why I read Rumi
why I look to the stars for solace
why the Quran
is just a book
and stars are my solace.
He takes me to his work
to make me stronger
since he thinks
my head is in the clouds.

The Clinic

We enter
through a dilapidated door—
me, Abba,
and there are so many
crying babies
their tears
could make rivers in the streets,
and women
heads covered in burkas.
I cannot see their eyes;
hands
that hold their infants
look rough and tired.

The Clinic

How can Abi
work here?
It smells like piss.
The wooden floor is splintering.
There are too many dark
and covered women
in one small room.

I feel
like I am going to vomit,
but I have to pretend to be strong
so Abi can think
there is hope for me to become the doctor
I never
will become,

so I pretend
just to see
the girl.

Ronit's First Glance

Who are you?
You could be my brother
(though I have no brother)
but not the way I feel
when I look
into those dreamy hazel eyes
of yours.

Arab boy,
with your gaze
my skin
slips off of
my heart.

Jamil's First Glance

Who are you?
You could be my sister
with your blue eyes
and the curls
cascading past your shoulders.

Israeli girl,
I know you are looking
at the muscles in my arms.
(I work with weights
most days)
which makes me
feel like a man,
something my Abi
laughs at.

Naming Things

I do not know your name
I see you somewhere
hands move like wind,
your smile—
slice of sun
crescent moon.

I've named you
talisman
for the wishes
buried
in this burning lamp:
to touch the bronzed calluses
that rise from your knuckles
to smell the aroma
of your unshaven face
to feel your body blazing
to dream
I can touch it.

Naming Things

I do not know your name
I will call you girl
with the song in your voice.

I am nicknamed Jordan
for the river
not a country.

These countries
separate us,
so I am banished
from the song
and the sea—
me.

Dinner Chatter

We talk
around the dinner table:
Ommi's good food:
hummus, falafel, baba ghanoush.
For my sister it is blah
blah
blah.

I hear Abi whisper
"he has a daughter
Jamil's age.
Can you imagine,
ever?"

"Never," Ommi says.
"Never."

Dinner Chatter

We talk
around the dinner table:
Imah's good food:
hummus, falafel, baba ghanoush.
Blah, blah, blah.
Too much blah, blah
while I think
about the boy.

I hear Abba whisper
"he has a son
Ronit's age.
Can you imagine,
ever?"

"Never," Imah says.
"Never."

Ma'ale Adumim (West Bank Settlement)

Where I'm from
the men leave for the holy city
while women make the kitchen
their home.

Where I'm from
the monastery of martyrs
once the most important of monastic centers
still stands—

a reminder
the past is dead,
though Arabs say
it is still their land,

forgetting
pilgrims once used this as a route
between Jerusalem and Mecca.

Where I'm from
I'm a pilgrim
since I dream
out of my mother's kitchen,

though my sisters
pray to my mother's matzo balls.

Where I'm from
school is our temple
(yes, there are forty synagogues)
but I revere
the God of knowledge;

we won
the Israeli Ministry Education prize
twice,
and a national prize
for our community's emphasis
on green space, on playgrounds.

I am from greenery
and recreation
on running races till my body is obsolete
on climbing jungle gyms
to grapple with—
what?

Where I'm from
everywhere I look
I see desert
long and sad
like a parched sky.

Two Selves

Where I'm from
trees
don't remember their roots
and hilltops
don't remember their hills.
I am the only son, half of a twin
who doesn't hear
the sighs of stars
or the hunger of the day.
I am from the love of school and poetry
from the river, words and sky.
I am Doctor Assad's son,
the one who lives in Ramallah
and East Jerusalem,
the holiest of cities.
It's strange to have two homes
and still feel like I have none.

I eat hummus and knafeh nabulsi
and listen to Fairuz,
while I play on my oud
and strum away
the sorrow.

Homes

I know he lives
in East Jerusalem
and Ramallah, both.*
If Jamil gazes
up into the hills
he can see my home.

We are neighbors
though he could never visit.
There is a checkpoint.
They would never let him through
without a reason,

so he must stay
down below
dreaming me
up above.

*His Abi keeps an apartment in East Jerusalem. This way he doesn't need to go through checkpoints all the time.

Home

I live
at the bottom of the hills.
She lives
at the top.
I could just climb up
to see her.
I can smell
the flowers in her hair,

but there is a checkpoint
which I can't cross
unless I have a reason,

but I do,
I want to shout.
Ronit
(I have heard her Papa say this name)
is my reason.

Ma'ale Adumim (Jamil)

I have named you
valley of the confused,
Arab and Jewish towns dot the hilltops
a bright sun shines
even in winter,
grass everywhere
and palm trees
hovering over concrete roads.

At the entrance to the city
two white doves
with the word "Peace,"

but the aged olive tree
is dried up in anguish
because it belongs
in my grandfather's backyard,
not yours.

Ronit

My mother, my Imah,
whose womb was a garden of gardenias—
golden girls
not sons to farm the land
but girls so strong
that make men move mountains.

She loves me, her firstborn
proudly and fiercely.
So she guards the fence
like a lioness
who could eat you with her eyes
if you dare to cross the land's casket.

Jamil

My mother, my Ommi,
whose womb wrestled with war
for years
until twins
tore through her womb
like a bomb—
beautiful relics
a son, a daughter.

My sister wraps my mother in solace
like a shawl,
while I am restless.

I am the eternal enigma
the Quran
can't answer.

Wolf

I have named my Abba wolf
because his hair is long enough
to hide his feelings.
I name him wolf
since there is something scary inside
ready to pounce,
a predator
but devoted
to his family.

The wolf in him wanders
over the fossils of his father
the fish,
my grandpa, my Zayde
the fish—
sometimes slippery.
But Abba
is different,

he always returns
to the desert
to his home,
and sometimes he is soft and warm
as a goat.

He gives his pills freely
to the clinic in Jerusalem,
"sad," he says
then adds
"he's Arab."

Puzzling
my Abba
the wolf.

Father of Light

My Father, my Abba
Aish Hamachelet[1]
not Eloheem[2]
though sometimes
his rage makes me feel that,
mostly he is Aviv Shel Kol[3]
and Aviv Shel Or[4]
until he discovers
Jamil.

1. Consuming Fire
2. Creator
3. Father of All
4. Father of Light

Tiger

My father is a tiger
sleek on the outside, contained
he pounces on illness
till it oozes out of you,
unless you die in his hands
then my father roars
laments, cries out
to Allah,

and my grandfather
snarls
"fool"
for becoming a doctor
in such futile times
for taking medical supplies
from the hands of Jews.

My Great Father

My Father, my Abi
Abi Alazeem[1]
Abi Hwa Batali[2]
Fel-youbarek Allah Abi[3]
but if he knew
how I dream the body
of an Israeli girl,
he'd fry me
in the desert,
still I say
Ana Ohibuka ya Abi.[4]

1. My great father
2. My father is my hero
3. May God bless my father
4. I love you, Dad

Imah

Why
doesn't she stand up to him,
tell him to leave me alone,
she must have known
the stories of the heart
one time,
enough to know
you don't always fall for
the guy next door,
though that is who Jamil is
(I have heard his papa say his name)
truly.

Ommi

Why
doesn't Ommi stand up to him,
tell him I have grown beyond the trees,
that I have my own heart
and that is what I answer.

Didn't she ever fall in love
or was that just a bitter pill
she had to swallow.

Zayde

I have named him fish
(though I cuddle in his arms like a cradle);
he wants payback
for the family
lost in the Holocaust.

He calls himself a Zionist,*
I call him fish
for the way he stays in deep waters
(where others would drown)
admonishing his only son
for giving out drugs
to Arabs,
smiling sadistically
drinking blood
for breakfast.

*Zionism: Jewish nationalism; the belief that Jews should have their own homeland.

Imagine: The Pharmacist's Profession

Imagine pills
like poppies,
sunflowers,
roses,
so many colors
in Papa's garden,
where people
plan a pilgrimage:
the Christians, the Arabs
always the Jews,

because their bones are broken
their bodies are battered
their heads are splitting open
like a bleeding melon,

and Abba's pills—
fragrant flowers
offer a promise
if not for today
for tomorrow.

When His Abi Isn't Looking

When he looks
into my eyes
sneaking glances
when we are at the clinic
and his Abi isn't looking,

I am the girl
who laughs, who is free,
one who wears skirts
and not pants, like I always do;

his gaze
makes me want to undress
so he can lift up
and see
what's beneath
the dress.

When Her Abba Isn't Looking

I have already left
poems in her pocket,
and she
blows kisses
when her Abba
isn't looking,

so I know
she thinks of me
as a man
who would lift her skirt
and love her,
not the foolish boy
my Abi
thinks I am.

Let's Meet

I hand him
a slip of paper
when Abba isn't looking.

My name is Ronit
here is my number.

Please call
so we can make plans
right away.

The Gift

I feel this piece of paper—
a gift
in my hand,
and pretend
it is her body
I am touching.

Call me.
I will.

Spices

"Abba,
let me get
your coffee,"
and he gives me shekels
tells me
not to be long.
I have already texted Jamil
to meet at the spice market:
the big one with tamarind, curry, paprika
every delicious taste
you can imagine.

"Salaam," he greets me.
"Shalom."

Spice Market

At first
we walk
side by side
our bodies barely touching;
I know a little Hebrew.
She knows some Arabic,
and as we continue walking
the narrow streets,
our bodies
are squeezed
together,
so we smile,
graze hands
and the smells of spices
hold me captive.
I close my eyes and imagine
the taste of tamarind
in her mouth.

Hands

Abi's hands
soft as dates
when he touches
the wounds of a child
swept from the streets,

but I remind him
"some of our people
wear bombs
on their bodies."

"Because there is no electricity
no running water
no health care," he shouts,
then adds
"our people wear bombs
because of this."

After
he wraps his arms, a blanket
around the burnt legs
of a baby.

He Touched My Hand

Smiling morning replaces frowning night
darkness stumbles out like a drunken man
Jamil's big bones startle my sight
if Abba only knew he touched my hand.

Darkness stumbles out like a drunken man
discover light inside his hazel eyes
if Abba only knew he touched my hand
my body rustles and it cries.

Discover light inside his hazel eyes
a cease-fire already taking place
my body rustles and it cries
dreams begin to run a race.

A cease-fire already taking place
between two bodies all ablaze
dreams begin to run a race
in our world's distorted maze.

Lightning Strikes

The first thing that I notice are her eyes
as blue as day or sorrow they have rage
she teases me to enter, my demise
if Abi only knew my heart is caged.

As blue as day or sorrow they have rage
from years of being told to stay away
if Abi only knew my heart is caged
a cacophony of hands that beg to stay.

From years of being told to stay away
the monster fence with signs "Do not trespass"
a cacophony of hands that beg to stay
how could I dare to dream that this would last.

The monster fence with signs "Do not trespass"
she teases me to enter, my demise
how could I dare to dream that this would last
the first thing that I notice are her eyes.

What I Love

Bones
singing over them,
dancing
when they are on the forest floor.

Imah
the light of her eyes
the lightning of her voice
she has taught me
to be strong
but in Abba's presence
she is quiet,
but he is a wolf.

I love the wolf
the way he cares for his family
his hands as large as leaves
and their shadows.

I love the drum, the whistle, the cry
archaeology
Where is his fossil from?
Jamil
I love Jamil,

I gave to him
with my heart
before he requested it
and would gladly give again.

I would kill him with such cherishing.

His bones
beautiful
like a bird's
ready to fly.

What I Love II

I also love
music
dance
forgetting
I have a body
thinking what I want to do with this body,
sometimes fresh
not like the good girl
my mother's made me out to be.

What I Love

Words
whispering over them
writing
filling up the page.

Ommi.
She worries I am weak
like a broken well
that there is too little water.

I love Abi
his hands like dates
sweetening our family.

And the souq[1]
where the kmaaj[2]
is soft
as her body must be.

1. Supermarket
2. Bread

Oh,

to take her to El Bireh

where there is a Turkish bath

NO GIRLS ALLOWED,

but I can dream

her body bathed in mine.

What I Love II

Disco
drums
dancing on the beach,
gyrating to thoughts
of Ronit
on me
in me.

What I Hate

Senseless school
like history
when they distort
that Arabs
have no right
to the land.

I hate idle chatter
my sisters rumble with it:
hair and makeup.

I like natural
hair like a forest of greenery.

I hate
when Imah asks me
where I'm going
like she senses
my subterfuge.

Lately she has been checking
my phone,
but I erase
my messages.

Does she want me to tell her
East Jerusalem
where the heat
is a murderer,
but I will go there anyway
heat
of his body
of my body.

I hate the parting
the sorrow of it
the fear
tomorrow will never come,
and I will not see him
again.

What I Hate II

That I have to pretend
that I don't know him,
how lame is that?

That I have to ignore
that I want him
now
right now
not tomorrow.

What I Hate

Senseless school
like history
that Jews
are the enemy
who robbed our land.
I hate the ruins
they call my land.
But what about
our rights to water?

I hate the way my twin
is Ommi's friend
the secrets shared
in hushed whispers.

Ronit's alphabet
its letters
are indecipherable
though she says
mine are, too.

And when Ommi says
"where are you going?"
the mask of her burka
a shroud for her face,

I want to tell her
the desert
where I can cross the bridge of her body
and feel Ronit's heat,

so much heat
dripping with it.

What I Hate II

That I can't say
let's do it now,
anywhere
who cares where,

that I smile
when I want to tell
my family
where to go,

so I
don't have to hide.

Ronit Goes to the Market

Imah
is curious
why I suddenly want
to do errands
but she is so tired
from the girls
she gives me a list,
and I go
to the Rami Levy market
where Arabs and Jews
sometimes mingle
and there are
natural foods
a bakery
a restaurant
Jamil.

Jamil Goes to the Market

A text:
meet me
at Gush Etzion Junction.
And immediately
I ask my mother
for a list.
"He acts like a girl,"
Abi says.

He should only know
I have a girl
who I will meet
at Rami Levy market,
we will hold hands
and kiss
with our mouths wide open.

I say nothing
take the list
and run.

Shell-Struck

They may have named me
"Argonauta"
Imah says
since I swam away
so fast
as if
every dwelling was temporary.

They say I have a land
but I do not feel
at home.

My shell
is feather-light
but sturdy, strong
compelled
by an unknown sea.

Jordan

They may have named me
"Jordan"
a pet name
since I am a river
my feelings are liquid
even before Ronit
I was the boy without armor,
because I love to read and write,
but I also listen to Coldplay,
so why say
I melt?

Are my prayers
too petrified for you?

Sweet Statue

I'll name you
sweet statue
with bronzed skin.
I'll ask the sun
to step aside
since the glare
is blinding.

At night
the full moon
reappears,

still
no one notices
"I am whiter than new snow
upon a raven's back,"*
no one sees
the full moon
and its treacherous treason.

*Romeo and Juliet, Act III, Scene 2

No More

No more
tender-boned
Jamil. No more.
So tired
of being the sweet boy
like a shepherd who
herds his sheep.
Soon I will be
a ram
who watches as
"the orchard hangs out its lanterns.
The dead come stumbling by
in shrouds.
Nothing can stay bound
or be imprisoned."*
Not me.

**Rumi: The Book of Love,* "The Music We Are"

Hunger

I am hungry for bourekas
stuffed with cheese
oozing on the plate,
maybe labane—
spicy or dripping
or jachnun
drunk with mint tea.

Imah grinds the nuts
for baklava
just like his Ommi;

then why
must I eat
alone?

Hunger

I am hungry for
knafeh nabulsi
the queen of Arabic sweets,
or date-filled semolina cookies
the magrood
of pistachio baklava cake,
and hummus;

my Ommi grinds the chickpeas
with the heart of her knuckles,
same as Ronit's Imah;

I am hungry for Ronit
and thirsty, too.

The Enemy: Ronit Speaks

My Abba has named you
the enemy:
the one who births bombs
and throws them out the window;
the one who would smile like a knife
just to see blood,
blood lips and rivers of red
for Israelis to swim in;
look at his eyes, they would say
they are black slits
(but he has light eyes)
and when I look
all I see is an invitation
to gaze at the moon
in your night.

The Enemy: Jamil Speaks

My Abi has named you
the enemy:
such a ruthless thief
to steal land
when no one is looking
change locks,
change the keys

(and I have the key
to prove my father right),

but when he tells me
your eyes hold lies,

I know he doesn't understand
those blue flecks are rockets
asking me to fly away.

Street Walk: Ronit

Yes,
I am coming to work
with Abba today
did you get my text?

Abba
almost grabbed the phone from me
and growled
like a lion
when I pulled it back.
"Next time," he snarled.

We will stroll
through East Jerusalem
through narrow streets
and small markets.

We will feed each other
nuts, fruits
oranges
from which
we will suck the juices dry.

Coffee
Tell your Abi
he needs coffee
with cardamom
hot and steamy
(the way I like
your kisses).

My Sister Told Ommi

Did not get
your first text,
since my sister
ratted me out.

I tremble
thinking
she told Abi, too.
His temper
is brutal.
He'd never
let me come
to work with him
again.

Ommi
grabbed my phone
and kept it
for two days,
but I had already
deleted the messages.

"I might need to talk to Abi," she shrieked.
"About what?" I challenged her
and finally
she shoved the phone
in my face.

Can you imagine
if she saw the message
where I said I wanted to eat
the fruits from your garden?

Coffee.
Yes coffee.
Piping hot.

From Her Sweet Body

I can't cross her fence
but she can cross mine
with her Abba
into my Papa's office
where he treats the poor, the sick, the hungry
Palestinian children
whose Abis can't work;

while mine
takes pills from hers
and I take vials of sweat
from her sweet body.

From His Sweet Hands

This barrier—
a thinly disguised veil
I rip through
with my eyes,
especially when Abba
brings his medicines
voilá—
healing happens,

but I am still wounded
waiting
for Jamil's hands
to help.

Ronit Texts

This fence
you cannot cross
you cannot see through.
It is 25 feet of concrete
will soon be 435 miles long
around Qalqilya:
the West Bank barrier.

There is no separation barrier
between you
and me.

Jamil Texts

This wall
is so high;
25 feet of concrete
435 miles long.
I can only imagine you
on the other side
your arms
swinging freely
in the summer wind.

Jamil and Ronit on an Afternoon Walk

Walking the narrow alleyways
of Zion,
eating murtabak—
Yemeni mutton-filled pancakes,
hearing the chant to prayer—
the Jews, the Arabs,
smelling the flesh sizzling
beneath the heated afternoon sun
and tasting it;

we are together
and we look like siblings.
No one knows
how burnt I am around her.

Shihab*

So be it
I am the shihab,
still, there is a sky out there—
Ronit
and what a fool
not to plant
in this garden of goodness,
discard
the seeds of hate
you have all tried
to plant in me:
my people and her people, too.

*Shooting star

Other Gardens: Ronit Speaks

"It is too rash, too unadvised, too sudden
too like the lightning"*

to call this love
the summer's ripening breath;

right now
we are flower buds in summer air,

but next time
we'll deflower.

Romeo and Juliet, Act II, Scene 2

Ronit and Jamil

Here we can hold hands,
walking through the narrow street,
no cars allowed.
Only
Ronit and Jamil,
today Ronit is an Arab
with her head covered.

Tomorrow
Jamil pretends to be Israeli,
and there is no separation barrier
between us.

Sun

Ronit is the fair sun in the east,
the one who kills
the envious moon;
I can answer her eyes,
but Chaim is looking
and though she may be bold and brazen
her eyes still twinkle
tempt me
to touch them.

Moon

Mohammed looks, too
even though I touch my eyes
to the ground,
he does not understand
the wardrobe of feelings.

I ask Jamil
"O, swear not by the moon, th' inconstant moon"*
because the moon wears a mask
while I undress my face daily.

**Romeo and Juliet*, Act II, Scene 2

Ronit's Kiss

"Then have my lips
the sin
that they have took."*

I will take yours
as mine,
and swear by you,
not the ambiguous moon,
or the dead night.

I will swear by you
because you hear me cry
and understand
the ruins of language
that stand in the way
like a contamination.

**Romeo and Juliet,* Act I, Scene 5

But then we kiss
forget night
and bombs,
forget this whole
confusing journey.

Light

Her eyes
are mine,
they light the oil
of lamps,
they are fueled
by fear
and longing;
they suffer
silently
watching the forbidden fence
between our people
and our bodies.

Keys: Ronit Speaks

I've heard about keys
ancient, cryptic
ones that have traveled
across oceans
guarded like gold.

No one
will enter
this house.
My heart
already
swings open.

Keys: Jamil Speaks

I've heard about keys
my grandfather keeps
hidden carefully
in the womb of a vault,

it once opened the door
to a house
on land
you love
but don't own.

ACT II

Complications

Ronit: A Walk in the Woods

I know a place
where there are trees
and the people
at this checkpoint
are lazy,
so we can walk the woods
and finger flesh,
not just
kiss.

Jamil:
A Walk in the Woods

I love this place
where we can hide,
but what if
Abi comes looking for me,
and I am caught in the embrace
of your beautiful branches?

Another Glance

I hold my palm to his
like a kiss,
my lips have the sin
that they took;

but his name
is enemy
though Abba calls him Jamil.

I know
what's in the shadows
of the words
he doesn't say.

I pray
for another name
aside from Arab.

Abba says
I can go on a bus
and someone wearing a bomb
could blow me up.

Jamil's family would never;
would they?

Homeless

I live here
this is my home,
don't call me
permanent resident
allow my father his doctor's rights
give him some benefits
not others.

Hundreds of olive trees
chopped down
burnt
uprooted
homeless.

How could Israelis
chop down trees
to build settlements?

Ronit's family would never;
could they?

Olive Garden: Ronit Speaks

You say you are water.
"My bounty is as
boundless as the sea,
my love as deep."*

But the land
is passed down
from my Zayde.

We can share it,
but don't ever say
I plucked the olive
from your tree.

Romeo and Juliet, Act II, Scene 2

Another Garden

Where is my garden
where is my secret Sinai?
my beloved olive trees
entire groves erased
uprooted by the contractors
who built the fence,
taking land away
from our farmers,

my landscape
obliterated
by the other side—
Ronit's.

Ronit's Text

You say land
was taken
from your farmers
to build the fence,
and olive trees
were uprooted.

This makes me sad.
This makes me scared.

Jamil's Text

I didn't want to make you
scared,
sad,
it's just when we talk about
whose land it is
as the rockets fly from Gaza,
and one lands
near your home;

I want you to understand
there are no answers
except for us.

No Work Today

Last night
a bomb
went off
on a bus
in Tel Aviv,
the night before
a rocket
came near our settlement,
so Abba says
I must stay home
I must stay safe
but my only safety
is with you.

Jamil

I got your text
and I hear Abi grumbling
so I knew
it was bad.

"They will retaliate,"
he shouts
and I knew
he was talking about Israelis,

I knew
he just doesn't get it:
our only danger, Ronit,
is when we are apart.

It's Complicated

This fence
I know it's wrong,
but so are bombs
people strap to themselves
blowing up our land, our people,
and the rockets
from Gaza
and the harsh words
in the winds of the world
that Israel is not a place
or a people.

It's Complicated

I am not a terrorist
not my Abi either,
I pray to Allah
to ban the evil spirits
waiting at the door.
Yet everywhere I turn
a checkpoint
so I can't leave
nor can I stay.

The Mount

My Imah tells me
King Solomon
built the first temple here
in 957 BCE.
It is the holiest site
for prayer,
ensures us there is God.
Sure
the Dome of the Rock
and large mosque
were built, too
in 668,
was completed
in 691,
but when Israelis won
the Six Day War in 1967
it was ours again
forever.

Dome of the Rock

My Ommi tells me
Umayyad Caliph Abd al-Malik
built the Dome of the Rock,
our people believe
in its holiness—
the Islamic miracle
of Isrā and Mi'räjj;

his son built the huge mosque
at the end of the Haram;

now
we enter our Mount
in one of ten gates
from the old city.
We pray
to reclaim
our place
in the world.

You Don't Understand

I began
in black stones
and subterranean waters.

Allah spoke to me and said,
"claim this soil
its heart
beats in your breast!"

I know the Quran
is just a book,
but it is here
the Prophet Mohammed
made his journey
to the throne of God.

You Don't Understand

I'm Israeli
I swear by my land;
it is my badge.
I wear it proudly.
It was the land of my ancestors
and in 1948
my Zayde claimed it
as his own.

The Temple Mount
is also mine
it is where Abraham almost sacrificed his son,
nothing
more holy
than this.

Not Just About

I'm not just about Rumi,
I'm also hip-hop
DAM
and even Ibrahim Ghunaim.
Really love "Min Irhabi,"
"Who's the terrorist,"
surely not me.

I'm about Ramallah
the streets
dreams of joining protests
my Ommi
has forbidden.

Protests
that say
there should be a two-state solution,
a home for Israelis
a home for Palestinians,

each its own state,

so we can walk

the streets

in safety.

Not Just About

I'm not just Shakespeare,
I'm Nico Teen
Asaf Avidan.
I'm music, moonlight, cafés
dancing on the beach,

and I might join
the street fights
for a two-state solution
if Imah weren't watching,
and didn't ask me about you, Jamil.
She wants to know
who you are
cringes when I say,
"Mohammed's son."

The Rockets

Rockets
suicide bombers,
blood on the side
of the bus.

Abba
looking at me
through slanted eyes
like he knows I have something
to hide.

Jamil

Checkpoints
work permits, not given
land
taken away.

Abi
looking at me
with angry eyes
like he knows
I have something
to hide.

Ronit and Jamil, a Walk in East Jerusalem

Finally
after days
of rockets
from Gaza
no casualties,
Israelis
sent gunfire
right back,

but here we are
holding hands
sipping mint tea
playing footsy with our toes

making believe
the rockets on the side of the road
are just pretend.

Ronit

I see your face
in the forest
its wildness
blends in the branches
of my body,

and this is it:
the enigmatic way
the twigs and bark
beseech me to enter
despite the fact
that I may not return.

But isn't that the point?

Jamil

I see your face
in the mirror
of the water—
sad eyes wandering
a lost fish,

and I say
this water is ours
no sign says
Palestinians here
Israelis here
stay away,

so I swim
toward you
and with you
away from the underwater's
ugly currents.

Ronit

I shouldn't
but I will,
I can't
but I must,
your politics
a plague
I have to stay away from;
there must be a better match,
yet I look at you
and you could be my brother
my friend
my lover.

Jamil

My head says
this is dangerous territory,
yet each night
the cloud of my pillow
takes us to a place
where your eyes and mouth
invite me
for supper,
so I stay
not away
my sister
friend
lover.

A Day in the Desert: Ronit Texts

My cousin will drive us
to Mitzpe Ramon
where we can shed our skins
at last.

Remember:
you're Israeli
if someone from the army
should stop us.

It will be
terrifically hot.

A Day in the Desert

Ommi says,
"you're going where with Caliph?"

"The desert."

"Why?"

"Just to see it."

She mutters
beneath her breath
and cries

"It is so hot
and there are so many Jews there."

Joined Bodies

We can do it in the desert.
No one will see us.
No one can smell us.
We probably smell the same
and taste the same.
Let's try.
Now.
My cousin says
she will take a walk
and swears she won't tell
Abba.

Land: Ronit's Ghazal*

A wrinkle upon the foot of my land
no need for shoes upon my land.

My holy forefathers prayed for this land
they wandered like nomads on their land,

now you dare to enter
on my land,

now I bid you entry
inside my land.

*Ghazal: A Middle-Eastern lyric poem with a fixed number of verses and a repeated rhyme, typically on the theme of love and often set to music.

Built of Bones: Jamil's Ghazal

There is nothing but the body
built of bones,

when I find myself beside you
I rise like bones;

from the dead and my desire
it grows like bones.

I dream of you daily
where I'm in your bones.

They can bury us together
and we'll share bones.

Water: Ronit's Ghazal

In such dry land, some water
while I dream of tasting your water,

my body withers in brutal summer
so what I need is water,

you say you're always parched
and yearn for water,

but if my body's yours
you share my water,

and if your body's mine
I'll need no water.

River: Jamil's Ghazal

My nickname is Jordan
I was named for a river.

My Abi doesn't know me
since I feel like a river.

These Jerusalem streets are hot
so I pine for a river.

My body is even hotter
so I cry for a river.

When Ronit invades my sleep
she crosses into my river.

Desert:
Ronit's Ghazal

There is a whirlwind of sand in the desert
but I find your hand in the desert.

My bones are brittle
until I see you in the desert,

and I am withered
but then I dance in the desert.

The air is hot and heavy
but I do not care in the desert.

My body sweats a storm
which I give you in the desert.

In a Tomb: Jamil's Ghazal

When I do not see you
my heart is in a tomb.

The whisper of your words
I carry in my tomb.

The shadow of your smile
creeps out from the tomb,

the warmth of your body
without it, I am a tomb.

If I can't be with you
bury me in the tomb.

Fences

You can't cross my fence
my land,
there is a fence
a gate
a body
that separates us,
but I can cross yours
walk the streets
like a coyote
a Jew and an Arab.

I dream
of escape
into the desert
where we look the same:
two bronzed statues
no fences
no land
naked with the sand.
Remember
the other day?

Jamil's Fear

What if I'm put in a tomb
and there is no air to breathe;
what if Ronit never comes
and I sleep with my ancestors' bones,
should I shriek like a mandrake torn out of earth,
should I curse this land
we both own?

Ronit's Fear

"My only love
sprung from my only hate!"*
That is garbage
since I'm watching
dates grow
in his land
in my land,
imaginary place—
our land
where petals pray
for hate to perish
where we drink mint tea
together
hours
in a café.

*Romeo and Juliet, Act I, Scene 5

Through the Window

Angry wasps
seek vengeance
under the cow-shed
in the red sky,
as Abi
grabs the mother
smothered in grief
while her baby wails
wildly,

yet I know
there is a better way.
Ronit has shown me
the nest opens
if you allow it,
and it is possible
to lift your head above it
and see a sky
without rockets.

Leaving: Ronit Speaks

What are the streaks of light
in the clouds
parting in the east?

Night is over
and day is coming.
If I stay here
I'll die.

Away:
Ronit Dreams

I've watched our letters
collide,
they are so different.
Your language
stutters syllables
in my mouth.
I can't always read
the bones in your skull;
I'm in exile
don't you know?

Good thing I know some Arabic
and you know
more Hebrew.

But now
I'm ready
to migrate
somewhere

anywhere

away

away

away.

Safe in My Skin: Jamil

Let's erect monuments
new ones
no more edifices of sorrow.
Let the sheep
dig their feet
in the sand,
while I have
dervish dreams,
am ready
to be home
safely in my skin.

Imah Knows

"I know why you run
to the clinic," Imah says,
"it is that boy"
and I say nothing.

Inside
I tremble
for the wolf,
my Abba,
who could
pounce
on Jamil,
never take me
to work with him again.

I cannot look in her eyes
for fear
they will betray me.

"If Abba finds out
You can forget it!"

Ommi Knows

"I know why you run
to the clinic," Ommi says,
"it is that girl"
and I say nothing.

What if she told Abi,
who has vengeance
buried deep
within his heart?

I cannot look in her eyes
for fear
they will betray me.

She grabs my phone.
"If Abi finds out,
forget it!"

Meteors: Ronit Speaks

That light
is not daylight.
"It is some meteor
that the sun exhaled."*

Don't leave for Sinai,
stay.
When we leave
it will be together.

**Romeo and Juliet,* Act III, Scene 5

Names: Ronit Speaks

Refuse your name
discard it
in the sewer,
and I will banish my name, too.

"What's in a name?
That which we call a rose
by any other word
would smell as sweet."*

Trade in your name.
Our skins are the same.
No one will know
the difference.

*

**Romeo and Juliet*, Act II, Scene 2

ACT III

Dreaming an Escape: Overlapping Voices

Dreams

Nothing is left of me except you.
Nothing is left of you except me.
—*Mahmoud Darwish*

For me
named for a river
feeling your body in the desert
you, the river
ordained to flow your course
into me.

For me Allah
protecting us
waiting in the shade of the olive tree
for my cousin, Samar,
to bring us to our home in Ramallah,
but this is a dream
its veil thick as a storm
Israelis cannot enter Ramallah.

For me, I live this dream
that you are here
with me in Ramallah
listening to the sounds of the stones
of my ancestors.

I am your ancestor.
We must be the same
the door has opened
out of the desert.
I summon the stars
to guide us somewhere
where Abba and Imah are not looking.

I know Abba sneaks looks
when we are at Mohammed's clinic
in East Jerusalem
when I disappear into a café
with Jamil.
We swore we were siblings
to all the gawkers
but don't you think
they knew otherwise
your hand on my heart?

This is it, I want to tell Abba
we are shapes made of the same parts
we belong together.

"Our weight has
become light like our
houses in the faraway winds.
We have become two friends
of the strange creatures in
the clouds . . . and we are now
loosened from the gravity of
identity's land."[1]

Ommi knows about you;
she reads me like Braille.
She says nothing,
but understands
it is not like me
to run to Abi's clinic
it's not like I like blood
or wounds.
I only heal with water.
I would rather listen

to the cries of prayer
fly out
to the wind.
I would rather
hear the birds beat
their wild wings
against the day.
The music of poetry
moves me, and Abi thinks
that makes me less of a man.

"I am the traveler and also the road . . .
This is my language,
my miracle, my magic wand. . . .
In the rubble of the enchanting world around me
I stood on a wind,
and my long night was without end."[2]

But what about the land
whose land is it?
Abba says I know.

But what about the land

whose land is it?

Abi says I know.

I celebrate today

when it does not matter

as I dream

the days

when we walked through the bazaars

in East Jerusalem;

did anyone really know

who I was—

my temple.

His mosque.

Today I dream

I am with Ronit in Ramallah.

We enter the Abdel Nasser Mosque

where mosaic is a mask

to cover years of hurt

years of pain—

Israelis feel

Palestinians feel—
I know we feel the same.

I celebrate our souq, our market.
We share delicious kmaaj bread
out of the oven
I feel the heat
of the oven
of the desert
of Ronit.

If only to take her
to the city of El Bireh
and our Turkish baths,
we revel
in the heat
of the water.

"We weren't stronger than plants,
except at the end of summer.
You are my reality. I am your question.
We inherited nothing
but our names.

You are my garden,
I am your shade,
in the final passage of an epic hymn."[3]

Today we don't hide.
We lick cones from Rukab's ice cream
here, where big buildings
and five-star hotels
line the streets,
where dabke dance
is just like Ronit's,
where film festivals
show movies,
where there are churches and mosques
and palaces, too,

where there is no fence
no checkpoints
no parents
only Ronit
only Jamil
and a house in Jaffa
and a bedroom, too.

Though I am an Israeli girl
I embrace your exile
I join the boundaries
of your body and their absence.
I hunger for your absence
and presence.

I am ready for you, Ronit.
"I wait for you with an azure cup.
I wait for you in the evening at the spring
among perfumed roses.
I wait for you
with seven pillows of a cloud.

If she arrives late, wait for her.
If she arrives early, wait for her."[4]

We are the night.
We are the lovers.
In Jaffa
we won't have to sneak
the way we do in Jerusalem.
Ronit says
she is ready to leap the fence.

Not just a fantasy of escape

the real thing.

1. From "Who Am I, Without Exile" by Mahmoud Darwish
2. From "A Rhyme for the Odes" by Mahmoud Darwish
3. From "Mural" by Mahmoud Darwish
4. From "Lesson from the Kama Sutra (Wait for Her)," by Mahmoud Darwish

Jamil's Dream

Ronit,
I hope you get this text.
I had a dream;
it was amazing!
I heard your voice—
Hebrew and Arabic words
we have shared:
how you embrace my exit
how you are my ancestor
and we must be the same.

We have been together
in the coffee shops
in East Jerusalem,
one glorious day
in the desert;
your flesh sizzled
in the heat.

I know your Imah said
you would get your phone back
in three days.

I hope I am not screwing things up
by writing you,
but I am sick
of dreaming.

It is time
to run away.

Ronit's Dream

Jamil,
I got your text.
Abba grabbed my
phone and threw it
I saw steam rising
from his eyes
"Where is that boy's message?"
"No message," I told him
since I had already
deleted it,
but here is my message
to you, Jamil,
I am done sneaking
beneath shadows.
I'm tired
of the subterfuge.
I have wings
on the back of my shoulders,
and I'm ready
to fly.

ACT IV

A Father's Lament

CHAIM

My daughter, she has marbles in her head
she says it's love, but no one is in sight
the day is done, has stolen all her light
she'd rather read and moan and stay in bed.
My wife she cries, her eldest is bereft
these months are like a dragon in disguise,
I feel her fire; she fills our house with lies,
it's not Ronit; there must have been a theft.
The desert's dust has entered in our home
the other children learn to stay away,
I'll take her pain and make of it a clone
my head fills up, oh woe! oh woeful day!
our garden's filled with agony and groans
please tell me, dear Ronit, what can I say?

Please tell me, dear Ronit, what can I say?
look at our land, that's bursting through the sun
I want a smile before you take your run
this constant talk you have to run away.
You speak of peace, but I'm a peaceful man,
you call me wolf, whenever did I bark?
Not like your Zayde, who you call a shark
I give free drugs to Arabs in the land.
I long for you to thirst, but not to drown
my cherished girl who wanders without aim
a speck of sand, whose searching to be found
and desert dreams are hidden in the ground
it makes no sense to say we are the same.

It makes no sense to say we are the same
no plague upon this house, but I believe
the message of the sword that makes us grieve
we all wear masks, but sometimes there is blame.
Imah struggles, yet leaves you all alone
says soon you'll be out fighting in the war
she keeps you busy with homework and with chores
her back is turned to melodies of moans.
Yet I cannot, her love for Arabs grows

it cannot be that boy, Mohammed's son
still Cupid's arrow hit, her body shows
Ronit grows thinner, I can see her bones
if it's an Arab, then there will be blows.

If it's an Arab, then there will be blows
Imah says, "You fool. She's scared to go fight"
the warrior will hold the gun with might
yet inside of her heart is still a rose.
She's always been a model for the girls
so smart in school, sews tapestries of dreams
when Chana* cries Ronit can stop her screams
a beauty, too, with gorgeous auburn curls.
I wonder if we're viewing the same child
I see a wanderer, a restless soul
the blaze inside her eyes is something wild,
and I am Chaim, protector is my role
my temperament is anything but mild
and I must help to make my Ronit whole.

*Chana: Ronit's mother

And I must help to make my Ronit whole
my wife picks dates, says what she needs is food
Ronit's a nosher, but nothing cures this mood
I think that it is time to set a goal.
"Leave me alone," she screams like a creature
"I'm thinking about math and of the night
when darkness comes, there is no sleep, no fight
stop with your speeches, you're not my teacher."
I feel the shadows over the dark hills
unwieldy, slow, heavy and pale as lead
I must get back to work and pay the bills.
Ronit tells me she has to go to bed
and all I see is sadness, no more thrills
maybe such sweet sorrow's in my head.

Maybe such sweet sorrow's in my head
but not when all she dreams is of the dark
to start a brawl, make certain of my mark
there is a chance the boy and man are dead.
I won't be deaf to pleading and excuses
a boy has taken Ronit from her home
as soon as the moon hides, Ronit she roams
not tears or prayers shall purchase our abuses.

To stop their love, before it is too late
for when he's found, their hour is his last.
I entertain revenge for all my hate
with hopes that with this poison he'll go fast.
She dreams him as her history, her mate
without a thought of history, our past.

Without a thought of history, our past
so much of family dead from war
aunts and uncles six feet beneath the floor
many layers of grief already cast.
Ronit has journeyed to the other side
in shadows where she whispers, all in black.
When Chana talks to her, she turns her back.
Chana seeks empty caves for tears to hide.
My little sheina beds the enemy
it does not matter that her parents bleed
however did he find the blessed key?
Inside our home, her heart, a lethal deed.
Jamil, if he's smart, has time to flee
venom's grown a forest from a small seed.

MOHAMMED

My son, it seems his head is in the earth
he says it's love, but no one is in sight
the day is done, has stolen all his light
poems and music are his friends and his worth.
My wife, she cries, her boy is so bereft
he dozes on his pillow made of tears
I'm struggling with patients, so many fears
Jamil in his cocoon feels like a theft
he's clearly in torment in day and night
indifferent to clouds as they pass by
on a camel traveling far away.
Jamil, your probing fills us with such fright
when we ask you what is wrong, you simply sigh
please tell me, dear Jamil, what can we say.

Please tell me, dear Jamil, what can I say
hunger holds our land inside its jaws
your mind does somersaults and questions laws
this constant talk, you have to run away.
There is no peace when we don't have our land
you question everything I say and do
Ommi watches your face and she feels blue
my heart is carefully vaulted in the sand.
I try to think that no one is to blame
for Chaim is my friend, and not my foe
my son, distracted, while I stand so proud.
It makes no sense to say we are the same
my hands, swift weapons try not to come to blows
but my grief about my people, that is loud.

My grief about my people, that is loud
when they are held as captives of the land
when they have claims to every speck of sand
each craftsman and his craft, he is so proud.
I hope you do not sway to hear that side
your dreamy eyes are drawn to mountains high
as if your spirit climbs and you would sigh
when Chaim's girl stands near, you're on a ride.

I touch my hands in hopes that I can heal
but there's no magic motion I can make
to bring my son back to my special view.
It's Chaim's girl who unearthed what my boy feels
his body bursts, politics he forsakes
his brain is shrouded; he doesn't know what's true.

His brain is shrouded; he doesn't know what's true
I'm busy treating patients and their wounds
when Jews are injured, my hands become the moon
since sickness is my sign, it's what I do.
If Chaim were my patient, I would heal
the treachery of blood and all the rest
ignoring prayers of Allah, I am best
in eyes of dust and gloom, I touch with zeal.
Yet so much death is smoking in the street
the earth she mourns from morning until dusk
the men, they wander aimlessly around.
The grief of all my people is complete
the spirit of humanity a husk
the heavy weight of sorrow leaves no sound.

The heavy weight of sorrow leaves no sound
the patients line the halls like goats in herds
Jamil's words sing softly, must be heard
voices of the maimed lie on the ground.
The sun at dusk becomes my enemy
with many more sick patients in the street
they moan sour dreams like animals in heat
while Jamil, my beloved, yearns to flee.
The children and their hunger pierce my soul
they dream about butterflies to take them far away
such dreams are myths on old, abandoned trees.
Jamil, my son, he sits in sorrow's hole
he's so entitled to be birthed another day
lacerations, deep inside, so he's not free.

Lacerations, deep inside, so he's not free
the cypress trees they limp across the land
the heat grows angrier upon my hand
Ronit has captured my son in her sea.
I wonder if they think that this is love
I need to shake the earth out from his head
fear fills up my nights, I cannot shed
I'll banish Ronit's sunrise from above.

Embroidered in my heart is this torment
must stop this before it is too late
behind the hills of very rocky rage.
The sky has ripped the flesh, and now it's bent
the valley of my soul is filled with hate
Jamil does not hear words from ancestors' graves.

Jamil does not hear words from ancestors' graves
he doesn't see our paradise is dead
he doesn't see betrayal in her bed.
He doesn't feel the anguish of the waves
Jamil has journeyed to the other side
where nightmares seek refuge all in black.
When Layla* talks to him, he turns his back.
Layla seeks empty caves for tears to hide.
My only son, he beds the enemy
it does not matter that our people bleed
however did she find the blessed key?
Ronit, if she is smart, has time to flee
inside our home, his heart, a lethal deed
venom's grown a forest from a small seed.

*Layla: Jamil's mother

ACT V

Onward

We have to go.

I know.

Abba says he is ready for the kill.

Abi says that, too. He's scary.

So is Abba. I'm not sure what he's capable of.

Oh, I know Abi has this ugly rage inside of him.

So why are you so sad, Jamil?

You're sad, too.

I know. My Abba, my Imah. Even though Abba is scary now.

For sure, my Abi, my Ommi. Even though Abi is scary now.

And what about my sisters?

My sister, too. We'll be leaving everything to be together.

Don't be so melodramatic, Jamil.

It's the truth.

What choice do we have?

Nothing. Nothing. We have to find another place.

Where we can dance on the beach.

Where we can just hang out.

Where we don't have to hide. I'm sick of hiding.

Me, too. How did it get this bad?

I guess they're idiots.

Ronit, it's not like you to talk this way. And it's our parents you're talking about.

Not just our parents. Our countries. The world.

Will it be better in Jaffa?

Jaffa might be for a little while, but not for long.

Why?

I spoke with my aunt, Natania. She is such a good doctor. She is the one who will give us a new look, but she says our parents might find us in Jaffa. She also said there has been tension lately. Israelis and Arabs always lived there side by side—until now. Lately some Palestinians have taken up with knives, and some Israelis have taken up with arms. Not good!

I'm scared of surgery, and scared of this fighting you are talking about.

Don't be silly, Jamil. Hair. Makeup. Dye. And fighting, forget it. There has always been fighting!

Why is your aunt Natania willing to do this?

She knows all of this is wrong.

Then why does she stay in Israel?

It's her country. She loves her country. It's the only place she knows.

But she is willing to help us escape.

She loves me more.

What if your Abba is suspicious and threatens her?

He would never do that. And if he did, she would never tell. Besides, she may not know where we are. Only your uncle Faaiz will know.

Faaiz. I am worried he will get into trouble.

He agreed to get us these papers. You said he has done this before. Given people brand-new identity papers.

He has. But I hate to lie.

Forget it! Live with it! What have we been doing these past few months?

I can't believe you just said that, Ronit.

It's not like we have a choice.

We don't. But I do not feel like a Jack.

You think I feel like a Rachel? It's so weird, it makes me laugh.

But I do not feel like laughing. I keep on thinking our parents will think we are dead.

I feel dead, Jamil. I feel dead when the rockets go off.

I feel dead when children die on both sides.

I feel dead when I can't see you!

Me, too!

Why are you so quiet now, Jamil?

What if we end up in America? Faaiz knows many people in America.

Gee, I don't know.

It has to be better there.

You think so?

Yes. It has to be better.

Perhaps.

Why perhaps?

America has problems, too. Every place has problems.

We can hold hands.

We can touch.

No country to contain us.

No borders, no boundaries.

Faaiz will make this happen.

Natania will make this happen.

Ronit.

Jamil.

Rachel.

Jack.

A new country.

Free of distant rocks that rage on angry grounds.

Hand in hand we can walk.

You, me, kissing outside of shadows.

It will be nice, Rachel.

It will be wonderful, Jack.

One day we can reclaim our names,

but for now,

PEACE.

LOVE.

PEACE.

AFTERWORD AND ACKNOWLEDGMENTS

THERE IS NO STORY MORE DEFININGLY ADOLESCENT THAN Shakespeare's *Romeo and Juliet.* It is not only a tale of two young lovers and their passion, but also one of adults whose blind intransigence serves unwittingly to destroy this love. In a world of feuding national and ideological viewpoints and territorial claims, this narrative renews itself with heartbreaking regularity and brings collective trauma to the painfully detailed, individual level again and again as a story.

So it is with *Ronit & Jamil,* my modern day retelling of *Romeo and Juliet,* which articulates a conflict between two families struggling, like all people who inhabit their land, to coexist when the convergence of their goals and claims has historically been all but impossible. This book imagines two star-crossed lovers, the Israeli, Ronit, and her Palestinian counterpart, Jamil. The voices of the teens may sound strikingly similar, a conscious decision on my part. The reinvention, coming on the 450th anniversary of Shakespeare's birth, demonstrates again the paradox facing every generation as it emerges in its own light: finding a future in full adult awareness while rejecting the burdens of the past. But I made a conscious decision for the teens to leave the burdens of the past behind. In this way, I selected to depart from the tragic ending in Shakespeare's play.

This book began in a village that grows daily. My visit to Israel and the occupied territories set this book in motion. My literary inspiration, however, was Elana Bell's wonderfully evocative collection, *Eyes, Stones*. In "Your Village" she despairs:

Once in a village that is burning
because a village is always somewhere burning

And if you do not look because it is not your village
it is still your village

In that village is a hollow child
You drown when he looks at you with his black, black eyes

And if you do not cry because he is not your child
he is still your child.

The idea of connections caused me to reach out to Sofie, my Israeli friend who lives in Brooklyn, and Talia and Yael Krevsky, her daughters, who provided me with invaluable research about the land, the landscape, and other relevant issues. I also interviewed a Syrian-Palestinian physician who practices in America, Lutfi Alasadi, who supplied his own perspective about the plausibility of this relationship. Sam Spitalewitz, another physician, checked my Hebrew. Lynn Dion helped me to think outside of the box, something she is very good at. Suzanne Weyn and Jacqueline Woodson have always been great critics and writers and have always supported my work. Hasanthika Sirisena, an amazing writer, critic, and friend, directed me to be a better researcher, and it is her belief in this work that allowed me to tackle the voices of the boy and the fathers. She encouraged me to start reading Arabic poetry voraciously, which I did. I also watched films: *David & Fatima, The Green Prince, London River,* and *Only Human.* The film that had the greatest impact was *The Other Son*, about a Palestinian and Israeli boy switched at birth, both of whom discover—quite by accident—that they belong with the other family. The sense of "otherness," of belonging to the same tribe, but the banishment because of the political landscape, was thematically evident in so many works of art.

I was very well versed in Western poetry and, of course, Shakespeare's work, but Hasanthika Sirisena's reminder to read the works of Arab poets propelled me on quite a wonderful journey, where I discovered not just the poems of the familiar: Rumi; Fady Joudah; Mahmoud Darwish; Naomi Shihab Nye, but many different ones: Najwan Darwish; Adonis; Samih al-Qasim; Elmaz Abinader; Etel Adnan; Sharif S. Elmusa; Hedy Habra; Nathalie Handal; and Mohja Kahf, among others.

Thank you, RF CUNY, for the grant that enabled me to complete this book, and the university where I teach, City College, for providing me the luxury of a sabbatical to complete my work without distractions.

This book never would have reached fruition without the help, support, and generosity of two remarkable people: my agent, Myrsini Stephanides, and my editor, Ben Rosenthal, who believed in the vision of this work immediately. Myrsini's efforts on behalf *Ronit & Jamil* inspired me daily, and once she handed it over to Ben, he proceeded to edit it with both care and passion. Thank you, Myrsini and Ben.

Finally, Ira, Samantha, Craig and Amanda, Ruth, "I am mine and you are mine" forever and a day! When I first started this book, my granddaughter, Ella, was just a dream for her parents, Craig and Amanda, and now she is real. Ella, this book is for you, too. I would like to think of this book much the same way, as my dream for something that can one day happen.